STEP INTO READING®

STEP 2

Party Time!

By John Cabell

Illustrated by Harry Moore

Random House 🏠 New York

It is
Squidward's birthday!
He gives himself
a new clarinet.

Squidward goes outside.

He plays

his new clarinet.

SpongeBob
is also outside.
He plays fetch
with Gary.

SpongeBob throws
a stick.
"Go get it, Gary!"
he says.

Gary brings

the stick back.

"Meow," says Gary.

Squidward puts
the clarinet down.

Oh, no!
SpongeBob accidentally
grabs the clarinet
and throws it.

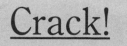

Crack!

The clarinet breaks.

"I'm sorry,"
says SpongeBob.

"You have ruined my birthday!" yells Squidward.

SpongeBob must fix
Squidward's birthday.
"I will throw him
the best party ever,"
he says.

Patrick will help.
The party will be
at the Krusty Krab.

SpongeBob makes
a delicious cake.

Patrick blows
up balloons
and decorates
the Krusty Krab.

SpongeBob and Patrick make a giant ice statue of Squidward.

SpongeBob wraps
a special gift
for Squidward.
Everything is ready
for the party!

Mr. Krabs goes
to Squidward's house.
Knock, knock!

Squidward opens
the door.
"There is an emergency
at the Krusty Krab!"
says Mr. Krabs.

Squidward and Mr. Krabs
run to the Krusty Krab.

When Squidward
walks in,
everyone cheers.
"Surprise!" they shout.

"We are all here to wish you a happy birthday," says SpongeBob.

"I'm here for a Krabby Patty," says a customer.

SpongeBob gives
Squidward a gift.

It is

a new clarinet!

Squidward plays a song.

Hooray!

Everyone claps.

Squidward bows.

Squidward thanks
SpongeBob.
"This was
a great birthday,"
he says.

Happy birthday,
Squidward!